The Girl with the Magical Curls

Written by Evita Giron

Illustrated by Rayah Jaymes

This book is for my daughter Tatiana
and all of the curly-haired girls and
boys around the world.

Love Your Curls!

This Book Belongs To

Have you ever
met a girl
with
*magical
curls?*

Curls so long and wild she could glide through the sky, use them as a springy jump rope, and even help at home with tricky chores.

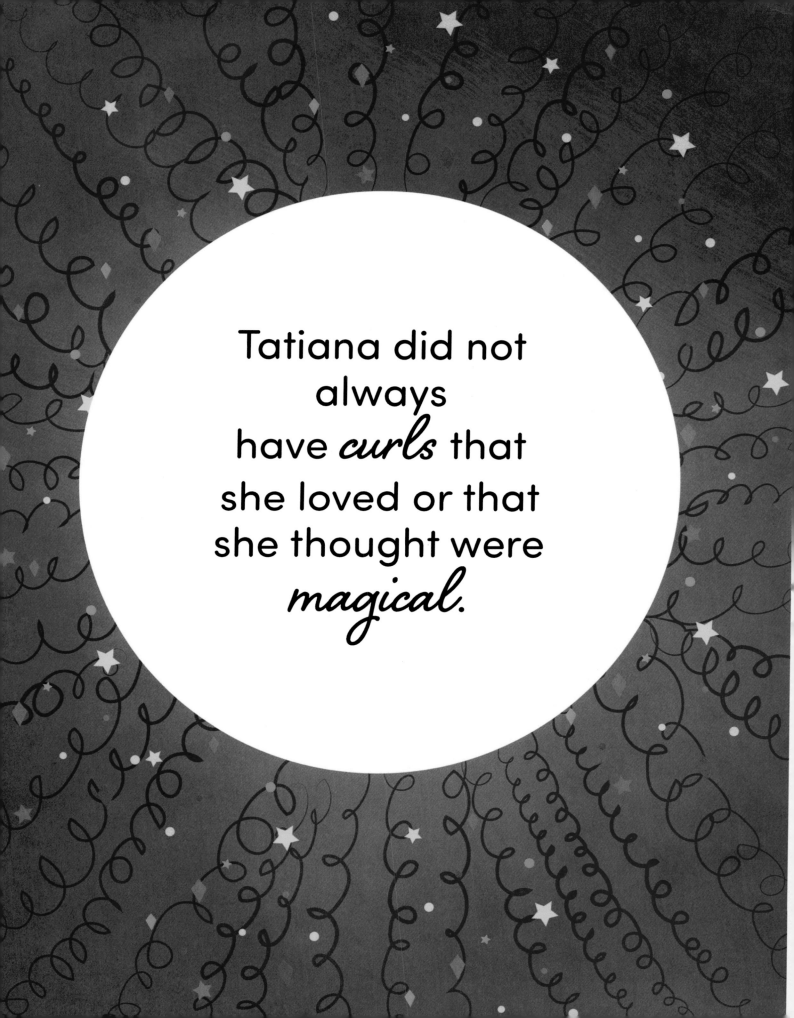

Tatiana did not
always
have *curls* that
she loved or that
she thought were
magical.

She did not want curls that reached high to the sky or were springy as a jump rope. She wanted long straight hair like her friends at school or the princesses she saw on her favorite cartoons.

Today was Wash Day, and it was time to go to the local beauty supply store with her mom to pick out new products for their hair.

Tatiana was never excited about **Wash Day**

simply because she did not like getting her hair wet with water dripping down her eyes and ears.

She thought brushing and detangling her curls took forever.

While Tatiana's mom searched the top shelves for just the right product for their curls, with a wandering eye Tatiana spotted...

a stand-alone pink sparkling glittery bottle. The bottle read, "*Madame Cheveux's* Hair Growth Oil, Just 2 Drops and your hair will grow as long as you desire!"

Tatiana jumped up and down excitedly and waved the bottle above her head, "Mom, look at this! I wonder if it really works!?"

"Just two drops and your hair will grow as long as you desire?" Tatiana's mom read the label herself. "I suppose we can try it on your hair, and even if it doesn't grow as long as you desire, it can make your hair even healthier."

As they checked out at the store and headed home, Tatiana began to daydream about all of the wonderful things the special oil could do to her hair.

"Now my hair will grow as long as Rapunzel's! **No more** wash days! **No more** detangling! **No more** curls!"

That night, Tatiana did not cry while getting her hair washed, or wince her eyes when water would hit them. She didn't even ask, "Are you finished yet?" as her mom moisturized each section of her hair.
"This is going to be my last wash day ever!" Tatiana thought while her mom detangled her hair.

Next, her Mom took the little bottle of oil and massaged two drops onto Tatiana's scalp.

At last, her mom neatly wrapped Tatiana's favorite silk bonnet around her head and tucked her into bed. "Mom my hair is going to be as long as Rapunzel's and you'll never have to wash it ever again."

Tatiana's mother giggled as she put Tatiana's favorite stuffed kitten on her pillow. "Oh Tatiana, your hair is not going to grow overnight. It will take time and patience."

Tatiana simply could not wait. While her mom and dad were asleep she climbed out of bed, taking the little bottle of oil in her hand.

she poured **every last drop** all over her head, and massaged her scalp, just like her mom did.

When Tatiana woke up
the next morning, she
rolled out of bed tangled
in a web of curls!
"My hair is longer than
Rapunzel's!"

"That hair oil was magical!"
She squeaked excitedly as she dashed to
her mom and dad who were speechless.
"What are we going to do with all of this hair?" Her
mother said already exhausted at the thought of
the next Wash Day with so much hair to manage.

"Maybe we can cut a little bit off?" Her dad questioned as he held up some curls as long as his body.

"NO WAY!"
Her hair whipped from her dad's hands and curled around Tatiana lifting her up in the air.

"It's **MAGICAL**!
My curls are **MAGICAL**!"

Tatiana could make her magical curls pick up toys, paint masterpieces and even help mom and dad around the house.

"You have been so helpful and responsible Tatiana!" Her mother said as she patted her wild curls. "You can take a break and play with your friend next door!"

Next door, Tatiana's friend
Catherine was amazed at how
magically long her curls were.
"I love your curls so much!" She
said as Tatiana's curls picked up
Catherine gently and tickled her belly.

Soon their laughter was interrupted by a loud cry, "Meeeeoooooooow! Meeeeoowww! Meeeooooowwww!" A kitten stuck high in a tree cried for help.
"Can you help the kitty down Tatiana?" Catherine asked.
Well, Tatiana had used her hair to help her mom get her favorite cereal from on top of the refrigerator, so she was sure she could use her curls to rescue the kitten.

With a focused look, her curls began to wind and spin up into the air, going higher and higher until they reached the kitten. The kitten gently stepped on to her hair and slowly climbed down the curly spiral staircase that guided it with care.

The kitten fell in love with Tatiana and her helpful curls. Tatiana couldn't wait to rush home and tell her parents what happened, and ask if she could keep the sweet cat.

"Can I keep him, can I keep him? Please!!! Tatiana asked.

"Only if you promise to take care of the kitten. Taking care of a pet is a big responsibility, and it was irresponsible to use the entire bottle of hair oil," said Tatiana's mom with her arms folded.

"She did make up for it by helping us with chores around the house," said Tatiana's dad. "Besides we could continue to use some curl magic around the house, and the kitten could contribute too! Isn't that right little kitty."

Tatiana's dad said while rubbing the kitten's chin. "Well, your dad is right. You did help us around the house and saved this kitten's life. I would say you earned yourself a kitten!" Tatiana's mom agreed with a smile.

"I promise I will take care of the kitten and take good care of my hair too!"

Tatiana said, while her curls danced with glee because of the good news.

Her magical curls wrapped her mom, dad, and kitten in a
big curly hug!

About Evita Giron

The Girl With The Magical Curls was inspired by Evita Girón's own favorite curly girl and daughter Tatiana. Evita grew up in New Jersey and now lives with her daughter and husband in New York City.

Evita also has a lifestyle, beauty and hair blog that is dedicated to celebrating diversity, multiculturalism, self-esteem and self-love amongst women.

Visit her blog site to find out more information **curlyvita.com**.

Made in the USA
Middletown, DE
12 April 2019